Jungle BuLLiEs

by
Steven Kroll

illustrated by
Vincent Nguyen

Marshall Cavendish Children

One morning Elephant went down to the pond for his bath. But who was there first? Hippo, and he was taking up a lot of space.

Elephant glared at Hippo.

"Get out of the water, Hippo," he said. "I want to bathe in peace."

Elephant was bigger than Hippo, so Hippo splashed out of the pond. But who was lying on the path?

Lion, and he was in the way.

Hippo nudged Lion with his snout.

"Move over, Lion," he said. "I need to get by you." Hippo was bigger than Lion, so Lion ran into the tall grass. But who was sleeping in his favorite spot?

Leopard, and he was snoring loudly.
Lion glared at him.

"Get moving, Leopard," he said. "I want this space for *my* nap."

Lion was bigger than Leopard, so Leopard ran to a nearby tree. But who was sitting in the branches?

Monkey, and he was enjoying the cool breeze.

Leopard glowered at Monkey.

"Get off this branch, Monkey," he said.

Leopard was bigger and fiercer than Monkey, so Monkey ran away to another tree.

But who did he find there?

His mama! He jumped into her arms.

"Mama," said Monkey. "Leopard is bullying me. He kicked me out of my tree."

Mama replied, "Son, you have to stand up to bullies. You go back to Leopard, and you tell him there's enough room for two on that branch."

But Monkey was still scared.

"He's big," said Monkey, "and he wants that branch all to himself."

"Then I'll go with you," said Mama.

When Leopard saw the monkeys coming, his tail twitched nervously.

Mama whispered some words in Monkey's ear.

Monkey took a deep breath.

Then he said to Leopard, "Don't you tell me what to do, this tree's big enough for two. Share it with me as a friend, don't be mean to me again."

Leopard whispered in Mama's ear.

Then they all jumped down and ran over to Lion.

Leopard took a deep breath.

"Don't you tell me what to do, this spot's big enough for two. Share it with me as a friend, don't be mean to me again."

Lion looked at Leopard. He looked at the monkeys.

"Okay, you can stay," he said.

He moved over, and Leopard and the others joined him. Then Lion saw Hippo on the path. He thought about how Hippo had made him move. He thought about Leopard's words. He got an idea.

Lion whispered in Leopard's ear.

Then Lion, Leopard, Monkey, and Mama ran over to Hippo.

Lion took a deep breath.

"Don't you tell me what to do, this path's big enough for two. Share it with me as a friend, don't be mean to me again."

Hippo looked at Lion. He looked at the other animals.

"Okay, you can stay," he said.

Lion and the others joined him. Then Hippo saw Elephant in the distance. He thought about how Elephant had made him get out of the water. He thought about Lion's words. He got an idea.

Hippo whispered in Lion's ear.

Then Hippo, Lion, Leopard, Monkey, and Mama scowled at Elephant.

Hippo took a deep breath.

"Don't you tell me what to do, this pond's big enough for two. Share it with me as a friend, don't be mean to me again."

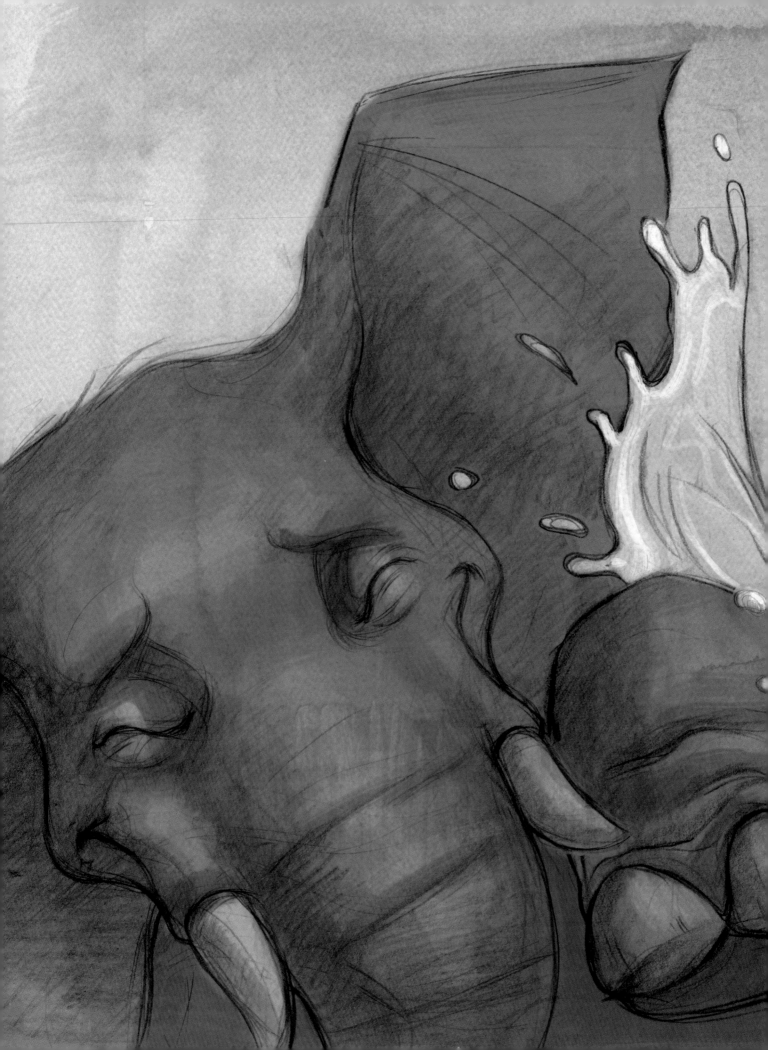

Elephant looked at Hippo. He looked at the other animals.

"Come on in!" he said.

Hippo plunged into the water.

Soon he and Elephant were chasing each other.

"This is fun," said Elephant.

"This *is* fun," said Hippo.

Lion, Leopard, Monkey, and Mama joined in, too. And they all said, "Big or little, large or small, this pond's big enough for all. Bullies aren't ever fair, it's a lot more fun to share!"

For Kathleen

—S.K.

For Mom and Dad

—V.N.

All rights reserved
Marshall Cavendish Corporation, 99 White Plains Road, Tarrytown, NY 10591
www.marshallcavendish.us

Library of Congress Cataloging-in-Publication Data
Kroll, Steven.
Jungle bullies / by Steven Kroll ; illustrated by Vincent Nguyen.
p. cm.
Summary: To get what they want, the larger jungle animals bully the smaller ones until Mama Monkey shows them
all the benefits of sharing.
ISBN-13: 978-0-7614-5297-3
ISBN-10: 0-7614-5297-4
[1. Bullies—Fiction. 2. Sharing—Fiction. 3. Jungle animals—Fiction. 4. Animals—Fiction.] I. Nguyen, Vincent, ill. II. Title.
PZ7.K9225Jun 2006
[E]—dc22
2005027072

The text of this book is set in Aldine.
The illustrations are rendered in watercolor, charcoal pencil, and digital techniques.
Book design by Symon Chow

Printed in China
First edition
3 5 6 4